Follow the
Setting Sun

To Carolyn : my
new friend,
God Bless,
Lucy Morgan
Waller

Follow the Setting Sun

A Novel of the Salzburgers and Ebenezer

Lucy Morgan Waller

WILLIAMS & COMPANY
BOOK·PUBLISHERS

Also by Lucy Waller

Let God Be the Judge
Table for Two
While the Coffee Perks

ISBN 9781878853646

This book is dedicated to the memories of Lucy
Murphy Morgan and Stanley Lewis Morgan, Sr.,
my mother and father; Harriette Dean Harrell
and Hewlette Harrell, my sister and her husband;
Joseph Murphy Morgan, Sr., my brother; Stanley Lewis Morgan, Jr. and Bonny Morgan, my
brother and his wife; John Otis Waller, my ex-
husband; John Morgan and Clay Vestal, my two
nephews, who died much too soon; and
to Stanley Lewis Morgan, III, our baby.

Contents

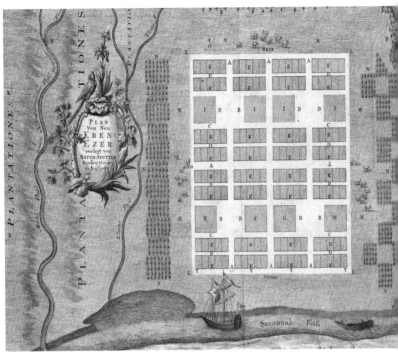

Plat map of New Ebenezer

Preface

FOLLOW THE SETTING SUN IS HISTORICAL FICTION. IT CONTAINS both real and fictitious characters and events. The Salzburgers were and are real people with a true history.

Some of the characters in this narrative—Pastor Boltzius, for example—really lived. He was the leader of the Salzburgers and controlled the growth and development of the settlement.

The dates referenced in the text are actual dates and the buildings are still standing today. The Jerusalem Lutheran Church still has worship services every Sunday. The replica of the orphanage is used as a museum today.

The cemetery does exist today. The family names on the tombstones are the same as those of their descendents still scattered throughout Effingham County and beyond.

The Ebenezer settlers must have truly thought they were following the setting sun as they crossed the wide Atlantic Ocean. Every night they could watch as the sun seemed to go down and settle in the new world. What a brave people they were to follow the sun to an uncertain future in an unknown but wonderful new world.

The Salzburgers arrive in the New World

Introduction

TWO HUNDRED AND SEVENTY YEARS AGO A SMALL GROUP OF Lutheran Christians set out on an eight-week ocean journey. They, like the Pilgrims before them, followed the setting sun, sailing west from Europe to the new world in America. Earlier they had been expelled from their homeland because of their refusal to renounce their Lutheran faith.

These brave people were originally from Austria. They called themselves Salzburgers after the city of Salzburg where they had lived. They had found refuge in Germany and were known as Lutheran Germans, adopting the German language and customs.

Not long after the Pilgrims settled in what was to become New England, James Edward Oglethorpe led those who founded the settlement of Savannah.

Savannah was just below Charleston, South Carolina. They had landed on the coast of the Atlantic Ocean and sailed down the Savannah River about twenty-five miles to find a suitable site for the new city.

Oglethorpe's group had been very successful in the new world and gladly welcomed the Salzburgers. Oglethorpe helped them to find their own place to settle about twenty-five miles west of Savannah. The place he chose was located six miles from the Savannah River. It was on a small creek, henceforth to be known as Ebenezer Creek.

The Salzburgers were very happy at first with what looked like a great place for a settlement. They thought the creek would give them safe travel back and forth to the ocean and the soil seemed to be of good quality for growing the cotton, corn, and beans as well as the Mulbury trees they had planned to use to grow the silk they were to send back to Europe.

Unfortunately, the first years at the new site provided more problems than growth. The topsoil proved to be very shallow and not fertile for growing crops, and the creek was bogged up in many places where rotten trees and other dead stems and sticks had kept the water from flowing freely.

Sadly, several serious diseases attacked the settlers. Dysentery was the primary culprit. It took the lives of the Salzburgers, the neighboring Swiss settlers and many others. Because of the many problems, after the first years, the

Salzburgers decided to move to the banks of the nearby Savannah River. They had rich soil to grow their crops and easy access down river to the larger settlement of Savannah. Their first home was known as Old Ebenezer and the new home, the one we still see today, was called New Ebenezer.

Today I live five miles from New Ebenezer. I have been a big fan of the Amish people for many years. I have read many of their books and articles and visited their communities several times.

I love the simple lifestyle and religious devotion of the Amish people, and I have wanted to write a book with an Amish background for a long time. Recently I was sitting in my car in front of the New Ebenezer building, where visitors come from all around to spend time. They learn about the first settlers and about some of the crafts such as basket weaving that helped them in their everyday lives.

As I looked around, I saw that I was just across from the Jerusalem Lutheran Church, built in 1769. It was the place of worship for the early settlers. I could see the old cemetery where many of the early settlers were buried. A replica of the first orphanage in America—predating Bethesda in Savannah—is still standing and has become a museum for Ebenezer.

In addition to these historic places that have been cared for all these years, the site itself is beautiful. The serenity of the place causes even the most excitable students who visit to speak quietly and respectfully.

The evergreen pine trees are tall and majestic. Other trees are beautiful shades of red, yellow, orange, and brown since it is fall. Many of the trees are covered with the hanging gray Florida moss. I couldn't see the Savannah River, but I knew it was quietly flowing a few hundred yards away.

There was an old cabin, one of the homes where the Salzburgers lived. On special dates Salzburger descendents come from all around to demonstrate the old skills such as weaving or making candles. At these special times we allow ourselves to pretend that we are here at Ebenezer, but in our imagination we are here with the settlers over three hundred years ago.

1

A Storm at Sea

THE TWO LITTLE GIRLS LEANED OVER THE RAIL OF THE LARGE sailing ship as the sun was setting. They had been on board for a week now and were beginning to wish they could be back in London or at least on land in the new world where they were headed.

Maria and Catherine had met recently in London and were thrilled to learn that both of them were planning to sail to America with their families. Most of the passengers were adults, and even if there had been room for them to play, there were very few children on board.

Both of their families were Lutherans and had been forced to leave their old homes because of their religion. Catherine's family came from Austria where the Catholics were in a majority and had forced the Lutheran families to leave their homes. It was hard to believe that these former friends could be cruel in the way they had treated their neighbors just because they worshipped God in a different way.

15

Salzburger
Lutherans
leaving
Austria.

Both Maria and Catherine's families had sought a new home for the last two years and had ended up in London with many other homeless Christians. They had been among those who had been offered a chance to join the group of Christians that planned to travel across the Atlantic Ocean to a new home in America. They were to sail to the English settlement of Savannah and continue with their own people, the Salzbergers, to make their own homes upon the Savannah River.

The adults had tried to teach the younger folks and the children as much as they could learn about what the future would hold for them. The Salzburgers were happy to have a chance to make a new home in the new world, but they knew that there would be hard times ahead.

Some of these hard times had already begun as they looked out upon the cold rough waters. They could see fish and dolphins every day and had seen a few whales along the way. They longed for a tasty fried fish as they ate the mush and the dried meat that made up their everyday meals on the ship.

In a place of limited space and things to do, the girls' favorite activity was to visit their friend Grandma Berta. Grandma Berta was from the same town in Austria that Catherine's family was from and Catherine had known her all of her life. In fact this midwife had delivered

A view of New Ebenezer from the Savannah River

Catherine when she was born.

Grandma Berta was not a doctor. She was a midwife, but she had some skills that a doctor would have and she knew a lot about the herbs that the doctors used from the nearby woods. In fact sometimes the doctors asked her advice about which herbs would best help their patients. She would likely be a big help to the Salzburger people when they lived in a place without a real doctor.

The children loved to listen to Grandma Berta tell stories about their homeland and some stories she made up to entertain them and ease their fears of being surrounded by water for weeks on end.

Late each afternoon most of the people would go down below. There would be a big room under the deck where they would sleep at night. The bunks where they slept were narrow and crowded and the air was stale and stuffy. The families would have their area where each family could sleep together as near as possible. The rocking of the ship in the waves would give them some comfort and rock them to sleep just as mothers had rocked their babies to sleep back home.

Most days were sunny and everyone liked to stay on deck. There would be light showers from time to time that would drive the older folks down below, but the children and younger adults would sometimes stay above board and enjoy the sprinkles. If the rain were hard enough they would find a wash cloth and perhaps a bar of soap and wash themselves and the clothes they wore. Since they only had enough water to drink, this rainwater made them feel clean and fresh.

One lady had decided to make the voyage against the doctor's advice. Her husband was part of the ship's crew and she did not want to stay home alone. She grew weaker and weaker as the days went on and, sadly, died while they were still at sea. Since there was nothing else to do with the body, they were forced to put her overboard in a burial at sea. They all knew that this was necessary if anyone was to die at sea and it was a scary thought for them all.

About the fifth week of the voyage thick black clouds

swept over the skies and the winds grew stronger, pounding the small vessel. The crew kept close watch on the upcoming weather and the passengers prayed as they, too, watched the nearing storm. Soon, they were told to go below to their bunks and, if possible, to use rope to tie themselves to the corner posts of their bunks. Mothers and fathers helped the children to settle in as comfortably as possible and gently secured them in place. Catherine and Maria each were tied to the bunks where they slept each night in the area reserved by their families. They, too, prayed to God for safety as the wind became more and more fierce, and the raindrops beat heavily on the deck. The ship began to roll from side to side much steeper than it ever had before, and everyone knew that it was possible for the ship to sink into the ocean taking all the frightened people with it. There was no one, other than God, that they could call on for help.

One of the older boys tried to prove how brave he was as he bragged that he would stay above board with the crew and help save the ship. As it turned out, the captain yelled that if he was to stay above board he must tightly tie himself to one of the poles that held the sails on the ship. This he did with the help of a nearby crew member.

The decks were awash with the sea, sometimes almost dipping into the water. The people found a new problem that they had not noticed before. The swerving of the ship made their stomachs swerve too, and some of them began to throw up. As the lightening flashed and the water crashed upon the ship, almost everyone was sick and moaning in their bunk beds. The children were too frightened to cry and one could see the stark fear on their innocent little faces.

One brave boy who had stayed above clung to the post that he was tied to. He knew that if he became free of the post he would be washed into the ocean. Like the folks below, he took turns praying and throwing up. The angry winds swept the water upon him time after time, and he thought the storm would never end.

No one knew how long the storm and the terror lasted, but at last the ship and the surging water began to level off. The raindrops became farther and farther apart and the lightening subsided as the end of the storm passed through.

The odor from the cabin below deck was unbearable and everyone who could move climbed up to get a whiff of clean air. There would be a long time before the bunks could be brought up and washed with sea water and the floors below could be cleaned the best they could. As distasteful as it was, the girls helped to clean the ship and they continued to follow the setting sun each day and pray that they could soon spot the new land.

2

Savannah

EARLY ONE MORNING THE GIRLS AND THEIR FAMILIES AWOKE TO the happy cries of "Land Ho!" It was a familiar shout for the crew, who had taken long voyages before and knew when to look for signs of land. They had noticed recently that an occasional bird would fly by the ship and knew that land was near. The Salzburgers were completely surprised and delighted with the news.

As the rackety old Purysburg faithfully pulled into the port of Savannah and struck her sails, everyone cheered and started to go ashore. The excited crew members calmed down a bit and remembered that only the men were to come ashore in the first hours there. The women and children were disappointed, but they came as near to the edge of the ship as possible and excitedly took in their first glimpse of a new world settlement: Savannah.

When everyone was allowed off the ship they found that they had been assigned to families who would provide a home for them. The women and children would stay in Savannah for several weeks while their men went upriver to locate and clear out their new home.

As it turned out this was a good time for those who stayed with new friends in Savannah. They learned that Savannah had been carefully laid out in neat squares and that each family had been given a small plot on which to build their home and another for their own garden. In addition there was a garden called "The Trustee's Garden" that was shared by all.

Savannah was a beautiful city with interesting people. Some people had come to America because they had been in prison in England because of their debt. Others had come for religious freedom or simply to start a new life in a new world.

Catherine and Maria loved walking around and making new friends. They especially enjoyed getting to know Hans Keifer who worked on the docks and came ashore as often as possible to talk with the girls.

The girls washed the few clothes they had every night. It felt so good to have a clean, neat dress to wear every day. Catherine brushed her long hair until it felt soft and silky. The sun had given it a light brown tint.

All in all Savannah was a pretty wonderful place to be.

3

Catherine Remembers

CATHERINE RAHN WAS ALMOST HAPPY AS SHE STROLLED through the small cluster of tree stumps near the bank of the mighty Savannah River. There were so many memories of the last five years or so since they had been forced to leave their homes in Austria. She still couldn't believe that they had been treated so cruelly by their neighbors and friends just because her family was Protestant and the others were Catholic.

The worship of God should have brought all people together to love God and each other. She would never understand how people could persecute others and actually beat them to death just because they worshiped differently.

Catherine and her family had been driven like animals to Germany where they lived for a short while. They had spent eight unbearable weeks aboard the small, fragile wooden ship called the Purysburg following the setting sun

Salzburger houses at New Ebenezer

across the Atlantic Ocean to the new world.

Like all of her family members and the others who lived near them, Catherine had nightmares almost every night. They reminded her of the loneliness, the fear and heartbreak they had endured when they would be forcibly separated from people they loved.

They had lived here almost a year now after enduring two years living in an unsuccessful settlement six miles away called Abercorn.

The small cleared spot was Catherine's special place where she went to be alone with her thoughts. She could have gone to the river or the woods or one of the other peaceful places. One of the advantages they had in abundance were the quiet spaces they could claim as their own.

Catherine lived in their small but adequate new house. The family shared the two bedrooms, with a sitting room in the front part of the house. In another area behind the main house was the kitchen and eating area. This separation of the kitchen and the sleeping space made the heat more bearable as they cooked over the large, smoky fire in the fireplace. The small outhouse was an adequate distance from the house.

Catherine grew a little tired and decided to rest a while by sitting in her favorite place—a low stump left from a huge tree that had been sawed down several months earlier. It was just on the edge of the cemetery and under a tall oak tree that gave it shade. Catherine often came here when she had time to think and ponder the last few years.

For a young girl just entering her teenage years, Catherine had many memories—most likely too many memories—for a girl so young. Most of her life had been filled with too many fears and too little security.

She had almost forgotten her best friend, Sandra, from her early childhood years. Sandra and Catherine had attended first and second grades together. They had attended a small school where they had learned how to read and how to count and use numbers to add and subtract. They had learned to be friends and to play happily together.

On Sundays Sandra worshipped God with her family in the Catholic Church while Catherine and her family worshipped the same God in the Lutheran Church nearby. It had never occurred to them that someday these different churches would separate the young friends forever.

Catherine remembered how the Lutheran men back home had worn pants that were similar to bloomers. They had big balloon legs that became tight and short at the knees. They wore colorful jackets that were not as long as a coat but long enough to be a respectable jacket.

The women wore long, colorful dresses. Some of them had suspenders and aprons. They always wore bonnets to match their colorful dresses.

Today in New Ebenezer they wore the same kind of clothes—both for the men and women—as they had back home, but the jackets and the dresses were not as colorful or attractive as they had been. Their clothes were made to be serviceable and comfortable and had to be worn over and over again, since the store of clothes they wore was severely limited.

Catherine tucked the bottom part of her long green dress under her legs as she tried to get more comfortable sitting on the stump. She closed her eyes and imagined that she was back in Salzburg again.

She remembered her father almost running into their home and calling out to her mother. From the urgency of his movement and the tone of his voice, Catherine sensed that something was wrong. She remembered now how that day had changed their lives forever.

Tensions had been growing between the Catholic families and the Lutheran families. Today a meeting between the two groups had grown from a conversation to a yelling match. Unfortunately, as the days and weeks went by the hard feelings and differences between the Catholics and the

Lutherans only grew worse.

Catherine remembered how her mother had begun to pack up as if they were going on a long trip. The items that were especially important to the family and those that held loving memories were tucked into small carriers that could be easily taken over the long, rocky roads if the confrontations came to that.

The memories now became so painful that Catherine would not allow herself to recall them. She tried to forget how her people had been driven from their homes and how they had to travel on foot for many months trying to find a place where they would be welcome. Perhaps another day she would be secure enough in her new home that she could look back and remember all they had endured.

For now the sun was setting in the west and she thought she heard her mother calling her name. It was time when the family would gather together for worship and a quiet meal. Another day was over and she needed rest for the busy days ahead.

4

More Memories

CATHERINE RAHN WALKED SLOWLY AMONG THE SMALL white crosses in the new cemetery. She was remembering the many events that had occurred in her young life since leaving her home in Austria several years earlier.

As she walked she studied the natural habitat surrounding her. Most noticeable was the long-hanging gray moss that clung to the tall pine and cypress trees. In spite of its beauty, it gave an impression of being spooky, especially at night. She had seen the older boys use it to scare any of the younger children who were brave enough to venture out from their cabins at night.

It was actually a beautiful place to live. The Savannah River seemed almost majestic as it swished against the high banks of the settlement. The ground was covered with pine straw from the evergreens and brown and golden leaves from the cypress and oak trees. Most of the ground was

The forest surrounding New Ebenezer

firm and hard, but fertile enough that it provided perfect soil for growing the beans, corn and potatoes that provided much of the food for the settlers. There were also sandy places and many spots of green grass. Wild flowers spread their colorful leaves and blossoms, further enriching the beauty of the place.

Catherine's best friend Maria was not with her, as she had to stay in and help care for her younger sister. Rachel, the sister, had contacted dysentery during a recent epidemic. It had been a hard time during which several of the Salzburgers had died. Rachel had been one of the lucky ones.

Catherine wanted to visit her older friend, Grandma Berta, but she was forbidden to do so. Grandma Berta was the nearest thing the Ebenezer settlement had to a doctor, and she was exhausted from caring for so many patients during the last few months. Back home Grandma Berta had been a midwife who mostly delivered babies. She, however, had acquired skills in using natural herbs and leaves to help patients survive some diseases. Because of her long experience she had knowledge of special treatments for symptoms of illnesses such as how to lower a fever in an emergency. She wasn't always successful, but she was always willing to do her best to help the sick folks.

Catherine allowed herself a few happy moments to dream of Hans Keifer. He was two years older than she was and they had met and known each other briefly when the women and youngsters had spent a few weeks in Savannah while the Salzburger men prepared a makeshift home for them upstream near the Savannah River. Hans had come to Savannah a few years earlier with General Oglethorpe's settlers in Savannah. He and his family had settled down in Savannah and planned to live there permanently. Catherine hoped that their paths would cross again, since Savannah was only about twenty-five miles away from the Salzburger settlement by the river.

It had been about three years since Catherine and Hans had seen each other. The Salzburgers had spent two miserable years in what was now called Old Ebenezer. It was a few miles away from the big river along a creek called Ebenezer Creek. The soil had been poor there and the insects had tormented the people. It was nearly impossible to get from Old Ebenezer to the big river because the creek was mired in underbrush and fallen trees. Fortunately the people there had been able to move to more favorable ground much closer to the Savannah River and begin to build their permanent homes in the settlement they called New Ebenezer.

Catherine was tiring of her walk through the cemetery and found a good log nearby where she could sit while memories and dreams continued to spin through her head.

5

Hans Comes to Ebenezer

SUNDAYS WERE ALWAYS SPECIAL FOR THE PEOPLE IN NEW Ebenezer, especially the children and young folks. In the hours before sunset on Sundays the teenagers and children were taught catechism in the church before the evening meal, but most of the afternoon was free for play or rest.

Sunday mornings were always reserved for worship. The Lutherans were peace-loving people and deeply religious. They loved peace and strongly disliked the idea of war.

In the absence of Judges the pastors generally settled disputes that arose among the people. Rev. John M. Boltzius was especially loved among the people. He led them both in spiritual matters in the church and was their community leader as well.

In the beginning at least seven deacons were elected

each year to oversee behavior. It was their responsibility to assure that all sins, including scandals or disgraceful conduct be avoided. They were also responsible for managing the money for the church.

Such was the community in which Catherine and Maria lived. They knew the unspoken rules of their people and generally felt happy and at peace.

This particular Sunday, however, was very special. The two girls chatted excitedly as they crushed the leaves beneath their feet. Usually they stayed fairly close to their homes, but today they decided to walk down to the river. Everyone knew that the Savannah River had a strong current. It was considered dangerous especially for small children who wanted to swim in it.

Although Catherine and Maria were now young teenagers they knew to stay a safe distance from the rushing water. It was nice, though, to watch the water flow and to imagine what lay upstream.

Today was special because of what would happen tomorrow. The girls talked often of the time when they had stayed with their mothers in Savannah after arriving from Europe. Catherine had spent much of that time with her new friend Hans Keifer. She had been too young to talk of love, but now that she was a little older she had begun to think of Hans as her special boy friend. The few times she had received notes or messages from Hans she knew that he was beginning to have special feelings for her too.

Hans had sent word by one of the men who manned the ship that brought supplies up the river from Savannah. The word was that he would be coming to Ebenezer on the next trip, and according to the schedule posted on the dock that ship was due to arrive tomorrow.

The girls giggled as they whispered to each other. It was quiet by the river, and the only noises they could hear were the chirping of the birds and an occasional call from other animals nearby. The flowing river made its own sound, much like the rain falling on a tin roof late at night.

It was beginning to grow dark and the girls knew they must hurry if they were to get to the church in time for catechism. They had a great respect for God and the church, as well as for Rev. Boltzius. They would never miss their religious instruction on purpose and today would be no different.

Tomorrow would be another day.

This old print shows traditional Salzburger costumes

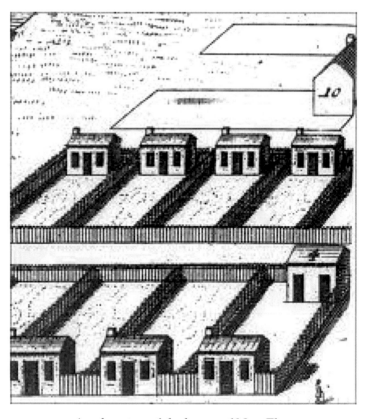

Another view of the layout of New Ebenezer

With A, knit 6 rows (gar...
Cast off knitwise.

Rab sur l...

Machine Washing and Drying: Wash in water (not exceeding 104°F/40°C) at delicate setting. • Do not bleach. • Tumble dry at low heat, at delicate setting. • Do not iron or press. • Do not dry-clean.

Laver et sécher à la machine: Laver à l'eau (ne pas excéder 104°F/40°C) au cycle délicat. • Ne pas javelliser. • Sécher par culbutage à basse température au cycle délicat. • Ne pas repasser ni presser. • Ne pas nettoyer à sec.

Lavado y secado con máquina: Lavar en agua (no pase de los 104°F/40°C) en el ciclo delicado. • No usar lejía. • Secar en la secadora a temperatura baja, en el ciclo delicado. • No usar plancha. • No lavar en seco.

6

A Day With Hans

BEFORE CATHERINE EVEN OPENED HER EYES ON MONDAY, she knew something special was going to happen that day. This was the big day that Hans would be in New Ebenezer. She jumped out of bed. She had laid out her best yellow Sunday dress the night before. As she carefully dressed and brushed her long blond hair she heard her mother enter her room.

Her mother had been preparing breakfast in the small kitchen that was separated from the rest of the house. She reminded Catherine that all of her morning chores needed to be completed before she could go to the river to see if the ship had come in.

Catherine quickly forced down a breakfast bowl of hot oatmeal sprinkled with sugar and glistening with butter —a tasty, quick breakfast. Then she went back to make her bed and straighten the bedroom before she began her usual outdoor chores.

It was brisk and cool this early in the morning. She hoped the weather would be warmer later in the day so she and Hans would be comfortable as they walked and talked together.

By midmorning Catherine was ready to go down to the river to see if the supply ship had arrived from Savannah during the night. She was happy and surprised to learn that not only had it arrived, but most of the ship's cargo had already been unloaded and was waiting for various customers to pick it up.

Several young men were still going back and forth from the ship to the shore carrying the remainder of the cargo. When she spotted Hans among the group of young men, she let out a small squeal of joy and then sat back to wait until he saw that she was there.

After a few minutes of excited waiting, Catherine spotted Hans running up the bank toward her. He grabbed her in his arms and gave her a tight hug. Each of them started talking at once and then settled down to normal conversation.

Hans told of what was happening in Savannah as more and more people arrived from England. He told of the news from back home that the new settlers brought with them.

Catherine talked excitedly as the two young people walked around the new homes and other buildings that had sprung up within the last two or three years.

Hans was surprised to see so many people going about their business of the day. Ebenezer had grown and changed so much since he was last there. He was so impressed to see the orphanage that had been built to care for the children who had lost their parents.

He was told about other places—Zion, Goshen and Bethany—where other refugees from England and Germany had settled in recent years. Mostly, though, Hans couldn't keep his eyes off Catherine and how pretty she had grown since they last had a chance to see each other.

The two young people walked toward the forest through the large stand of Mulberry trees that the settlers had planted. Catherine told Hans how the Salzburgers had agreed to help General Oglethorpe's people in Savannah grow the trees to give a home to the silkworms that would provide silk to be sent back to England. Hans laughed a little about the silkworms because this was nothing new to him. His people, too, were trying to grow the Mulberry trees and produce the silk for England.

Just beyond the Mulberry trees was a small cabin where

Grandma Berta lived. She had gotten to know Hans and his people when they all were in Savannah waiting for the men to come back and take them to Ebenezer. She had heard that Hans was coming for a quick visit and was anxiously awaiting them.

Grandma Berta had not left Austria because she had been ordered to leave, like so many of the others had. She left to be with her friends and for the adventure. Not only was she a welcome friend, but also was an experienced midwife and a self-taught doctor. She went into the forest and collected herbs and roots that could be used to quiet a fever or help the sick breathe more easily. She was able to do many things to help sick people that most of the people did not know about.

Grandma Berta was like a walking history book. The people were not able to bring most of their books from home, and the history and knowledge that they heard from Grandma Berta was very important to them. Catherine visited Grandma Berta often and listened for hours at a time to the things she had to tell. Today she and Hans just paid a visit to the old lady and enjoyed her company.

Hans, in turn, was happy to share with Catherine and Grandma Berta news he brought from Savannah. He told about two young brothers who were Methodist preachers.

They were John and Charles Wesley, who were responsible for starting the first Methodist Church in Savannah.

Catherine and Hans found stumps in the forest to sit and talk. Each shared stories about their daily lives and about the amazing growth of the new world they each had become a part of. They were too young yet to even speak of love, but Hans let his lips brush softly over hers, and their eyes gave promise that they would see each other again.

As they walked back to the ship Catherine decided to share a remarkable thing that she had recently heard from a small group of Creek Indians who lived nearby. She had gone with her father and Chief Tomochichi to visit and take supplies to the Indians. She could not speak their language, but Tomochichi, who understood both languages, translated for her and her father.

It was a story that some people had trouble believing. Catherine and her father listened carefully, and neither could tell what the other one was thinking. Tomochichi slowly explained to them that what he would tell was considered a legend among the Indians. They were known for their legends and many of them were made up to explain the things they knew about but could not understand. Since they had been cut off from the rest of the world by the oceans on either side of America they had missed out on what had happened elsewhere. Even their religion worshipped their idea of God, but they did not have bibles to teach them about the true God.

They told of a legend that they had heard all of their lives. It had been part of their culture for thousands of years. According to the legend there had been a white man who walked among them at one time. He was the only white man that had been seen in America until the time of Columbus. The Indians at that time did not even know that white people who were different from themselves existed.

They had no idea how this young white man had gotten to where they lived or where he had come from. They marvelled at the fact that he could speak the language of the people wherever he visited.

The man showed the Indians scars that he bore in his hands and his feet. He also shared what had once been a deep gash in his side.

Not only did he visit the Indians, but the legend of his visit was not for the Creek alone. At some time in the past each tribe had its own version of the white man who walked the Americas.

They learned from him about his heavenly father and how the world had been created. They learned from him what the newcomers believed about him and his cruel death on the cross. Most of the Indians in America had believed the good news that this stranger shared about God. They had learned to worship the true God, and they listened eagerly now that other white men and women from the lands of the rising sun shared the truth about God with them.

This was the first time that Hans had heard of this legend from the Indian tribes, but he immediately recognized the strange white man with the scars in his hands and feet. Once again he listened in awe about the Lord he worshiped and the reason his people had followed the setting sun to the new world.

There was so much to share for Catherine and Hans about themselves and their people. Hans promised that he would return to Ebenezer as soon as he could arrange passage on one of the ships coming from Savannah. Catherine's father had promised that someday he would take Catherine with him when he had to go to Savannah for supplies. It might be months or it might be years, but it was a promise that both young people clung to as they sadly waved to each other as the ship sailed out of sight.

Salzburger house and well

7

Little Boy Lost

CATHERINE HAD BEEN ALLOWED TO SLEEP A LITTLE LATER than usual today. She was awakened by a noise that resembled the scream of a frightened tiger. She had never heard a sound that terrified her as this one did. It took what seemed like a long time for her body to be able to move.

She ran toward the parlor and saw her parents looking out the front door. They, too, were still and reminded her of her father's expression, "scared stiff." Her mother was the first one to speak. She said that Mrs. Zeigler from two houses down was the one making the noise and running around and around. Catherine's family joined several other families hurrying toward Mrs. Zeigler.

"Johann, Johann," the frightened mother called over and over. Pastor Boltzius had heard her from the nearby church where he was working and walked slowly over to the distraught lady. He gently laid his arm around her waist and drew her toward her home.

For several long minutes everyone stood still, and from the lip movements most of them seemed absorbed in prayer. Whatever the problem that had upset Mrs. Zeigler surely needed the touch of prayer.

As Pastor Boltzius left the Zeigler home everyone gathered as near as they could and listened as he explained what had happened. Most of the people had not noticed that some of the men, including Mr. Zeigler, were missing from the group. Now they would learn why and where they had gone.

Around daybreak, they learned, Mrs. Zeigler had taken Johann and her older son, Jacob ,with her into the edge of the woods to look for blackberries. She was hungry for a blackberry pie and in a few hours it would be too hot to venture out to look for them. They had come upon a large clump of blackberries, and she and Jacob were happily putting the large juicy berries into the basket they shared.

After just a few minutes the mother announced to Jacob that the basket was full and they should return home. She called to Johann and waited for him to come to her.

As they called they walked down the path they had used to go into the woods. As they walked the calling became louder and the walking became faster. Jacob was sent home to get his father to help search for Johann. Neighbors who lived near the woods came out to look as well. As time went by the parents became more and more frantic.

Now Pastor Boltzius asked everyone who was able to join the men in the woods while he stayed with the distraught mother and helped her pray to God to bring their son safely home.

The searchers spread out and went farther and farther into the woods. They carefully examined the crevices that were large enough for a small boy to fall into. They looked for any sign of clothing the boy had worn that morning. They made sure there were no tracks or other signs that wild animals had been in the area. So many things could have happened to a small boy, and none of them was good.

As darkness began to fall, most of the exhausted searchers went home to rest. The few who were able to continue promised to keep looking throughout the night while the others promised to return at the first light the next day. Everyone who came to or passed through Ebenezer was told about the missing child and asked to be on lookout for him as they travelled back and forth to Savannah or other nearby settlements.

As time passed the men and women of Ebenezer had to

return to their daily lives. They continued to clear the land, plant the crops, and help build new homes as fellow Lutherans arrived and joined their group.

The Zeigler family continued to weep for their lost child. Someone constructed a small white cross in the cemetery with the name *Johann Zeigler* painted on it. They all agreed that wherever his little body was might never be known, but surely his soul and his spirit were with Jesus and that he would be reunited with his family someday.

8

What Happened to Johann?

LITTLE JOHANN ZEIGLER WAS ONLY THREE YEARS OLD. HE HAD lived all of his life in Ebenezer with his family. He had the prettiest blue eyes and light blonde hair. His smooth skin was tanned from playing out in the sun every day. All he knew of the big world that God had created was the small settlement where he lived.

On the day of his disappearance his mother had awakened him and his big brother as the sun's rays were just creeping through the bedroom window. She had a woven basket in her left hand and the little outfit that Johann had worn last night. She quietly helped Johann dress and handed him a fat round biscuit with strawberry jelly she had made the day before. She told the boys that she was hungry for a blackberry pie and that she knew where a big patch of berries was hiding in the nearby woods.

She knew how Johann liked a new adventure and how he especially liked to explore in the woods. She thought he could explore nearby while she and his older brother picked the juicy berries.

Johann was still sleepy, but he was beginning to see all the pretty plants around him and decided to follow a small brown bunny that came bouncing by. The bunny soon disappeared into a small hole which Johann could not see into or encourage the bunny to come out and play. On his own Johann started to follow what looked like a narrow path into the woods. He could hear the morning sounds of the woods animals, and he stopped to pick some of the pretty wild flowers for his mother.

By this time mother had gathered enough berries and began to call for Johann to come home with her and his brother. Neither mother nor Johann realized how far he had wandered and that he could no longer hear her voice. He ran faster and yelled louder for what seemed to be a very long time. He was at last so exhausted that he stumbled upon a grassy spot where he lay down and gasped for air.

By now the screams had turned to sobs and Johann was truly afraid. He did not hear the strange men on horseback until they were upon him. They were talking in a strange language. Johann did not know that there were people who were natives to America or that his people usually called them Indians. Their clothes were not made from cloth like Johann's and they wore only the strange-shaped pants below their waists. The top part of their bodies was bare, and some of them had designs painted on them. Most of them had long black hair and stern dark eyes.

One of the men gently scooped Johann up and placed him on his horse in front of himself. With a soft command the man gave directions for all the other men to start to ride. Johann did not know how long they rode, but it seemed like a very long way. He was afraid they had gone too far to be taking him back to his mother as he had thought at first. He wanted to close his tired eyes and go to sleep, but he in his own childish way could not trust the strangers who had taken him. Surely the next day they would take him home.

Savannah River seen from the site of New Ebenezer

9

A True Brave

LITTLE JOHANN RUBBED HIS SLEEPY EYES AS HE TRIED TO SIT UP
on his warm blanket. At first he couldn't remember the
events of the day before and started to call for his mother.
He was frightened when he didn't recognize his surround-
ings until he spotted Nahuna lying on a larger blanket
across the room from him. Now he remembered and knew
that today would be the day they would take him home.

Upon hearing his movement Nahuna quietly arose
and came to give the little boy a warm hug and a greet-
ing that must have meant "good morning." He watched
as she dipped from the same pot he had eaten from last
night and was glad when she took the bowl close to the
fire for it to heat up. In a few minutes she placed the bowl
of warm corn mush in front of him, and this time she
also gave him a small piece of fried fish. He didn't know

how to say "thank you," but she could see from the way he made quick work of eating the breakfast that he appreciated it. He hoped that she would offer him a second helping, but instead she helped him up and slipped a small pair of brown leather short pants over his underpants from home. The new pants were identical to the ones he had seen on the other young boys of the tribe. He waited for her to give him a shirt to go with the pants, but then remembered that the Indian boys did not wear anything on the top part of their bodies. It made him shiver a bit, knowing that he was not to wear a shirt today.

As the day went on Johann admitted to himself that he would not be going home today. In fact he would not go home for a long time. The days turned into weeks and they in turn turned into months and years. As the time went by it became harder and harder for the child to remember that he was different, that Nahuna was not his real mother and that the chief was not his real grandfather. Still, he daily promised himself that as soon as he was old enough he would run away and find his own way back to his real family.

Nahuna was very kind to Johann. She grew to love him very much as if she had been his real mother, and he loved her too. He called her Mama. They did not know the

English word, but they were pretty sure of its meaning. The other boys taught him their games and played well with him. Nahuna's father taught him the Indian ways and how to make the tools and other things he would need. Like all the boys in the tribe he learned to hunt and fish to provide food for the family.

When Johann was about to turn twelve years old he was called to his Indian grandfather's home for a special talk about how he would soon be becoming a young man. The Indians carried out a "right of passage" ceremony for each young boy as he approached his twelfth birthday.

Along with the ceremony the boy would be given a chance to prove how brave he was and to claim the right to become a man.

Johann listened carefully as Grandfather talked. He had never been known as a coward, but for the first time he was beginning to wonder if he would be able to really prove how brave he was. He had known other boys who had gone through the "right of passage," but they had been very secretive about what had happened to them. Grandfather explained that the two of them (Grandfather and Johann) would go deep into the forest. They would find a stump where Johann would have to sit all night. It would be dark and scary, and he would have to wear a blindfold over his eyes. He would have to listen to the sounds of the bears and wolves and other wild animals, and he would feel the blowing wind and maybe the sharp drops of a rainstorm. He would hear the thunder and lightning, but he could not remove his blindfold throughout the long night. Johann could not believe that Grandfather would desert him to spend the night in terror all alone. He did so want Grandfather to be proud of him, but it was hard to keep back the tears as Grandfather placed the blindfold on Johann's face and walked away.

Johann tried desperately to remember his home with his real family. He wanted more than anything to jerk off the hated blindfold and start to run through the forest in the hope that he could find his way back to his people. He remembered one of his friends who had set out with his father for the night and had returned to the village long before morning. Now Johann understood why all the men had shunned him and refused to let him meet with the men of the tribe. It was such a disgrace, and in spite of his fear Johann did not want his grandfather to be ashamed of him.

He was getting a little sleepy and beginning to grow calmer when he heard heavy footsteps stomping through the thin, dry leaves. It sounded like someone walking toward him, but he knew no one was around. No person that is, but a mind-chilling roar reminded him that huge bears ruled this part of the forest. He wondered what it was going to feel like when the sharp teeth plunged into his chest. He wondered how long it would take for death to come and rescue him from the bear's claws.

His hand was moving toward his blindfold. At least he would be able to see the final minutes of his young life. But then the roaring stopped, and as he listened the footsteps seemed to be going in the opposite direction. His body shook so hard it took a real effort to catch his breath. He realized he was exhausted and sat numbly for the rest of the night.

This time he again heard footsteps coming toward him, but with them he heard the welcome sound of Grandfather's voice. As he removed the blindfold for the last time, Grandfather gave him a big hug and gently took his hand as they walked proudly back to the village. Two years later Johann learned that Grandfather had spent the night standing at his side and that he had scared the bear away to protect his special young brave. He had always thought his adopted Grandfather loved him and now he knew for sure that he did.

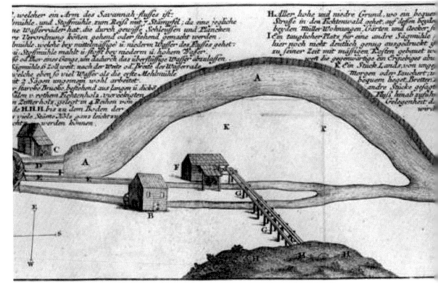

Drawing showing the water mill at Ebenezer

10

Anna Finds a Home

Time went on for the Salzburgers at the Ebenezer Settlement. The children grew up and new babies were born. Many newcomers—both Salzburgers and others—moved to the area. Some of them settled in Ebenezer and made a new life for themselves and others moved on to the growing settlements in other parts of the new land.

Sadly many of the folks in Ebenezer died young. Some died from illnesses and others from accidents or other causes. They did have a doctor, but sometimes he did not have the knowledge or experience to help those who needed more medical care.

Anna Huber, who had moved to the orphanage after losing her parents and siblings soon after coming to America, was often seen sitting on the front steps of the orphanage. She looked sad, as if she was remembering her family and longing for a family of her own.

Mrs. Zeigler bore the same sad look as she remembered her three-year-old son Johann who had disappeared into the woods and had not been seen since.

Sometimes Mrs. Zeigler would stop to comfort Anna, and she found that the girl shared her feelings and comforted her as well. Anna would share memories of her family, and Mrs. Zeigler would tell her about little Johann. There were times when Anna would be invited to visit the Zeigler family or have a meal with them. She enjoyed playing with the Zeigler boys, Jacob and Joshua.

By this time the orphanage had more children than it actually had room for. Because they loved these children and there was nowhere else for them to live, they never turned a child away. They learned to live under crowded conditions and sometimes allowed one or more of the children to be adopted by another family. This is how Anna became a part of the Zeigler family.

Often small groups of Creek Indians who had always lived nearby passed through Ebenezer on their way to the Savannah River. Some of them had learned to speak English and would stop and trade with the white settlers. The Indians taught their new neighbors how to fertilize their crops, especially the popular corn crop. They used dead fish to plant with the corn and give it a more abundant yield. The white people had learned to share their knowledge of farming with the Indians. They also traded tools and other goods they had brought from England.

Occasionally other tribes from farther away would pass nearby to find a way to the river. They were a little more frightening than the Creek, but had never harmed any of the people of Ebenezer.

Early one morning in mid summer a small group of these Indians found themselves surrounded by the light -skinned strangers. Most of them did not speak English or German and were afraid. One tall, dark Indian who seemed to be the leader pulled ahead and indicated that he could communicate with them. He was followed by a teen-aged boy who might have been his son.

This strange man, as well as the boy, spoke bits of English. It was enough to keep each group of strangers from harming the other. In fact since the Indians looked so tired and hungry they were asked to step down from their horses and share a bit of the food the families were eating.

The young boy had not moved from his saddle. He seemed to be mesmerized with the buildings and the people around him. Likewise, one lady among the Salz-burgers stood to the side of the crowd without her usual meaningless chatter.

There was a bond between the lady and the teenager that neither of them understood at first. It wasn't until her son, Jacob, came to her that she saw the resemblance between Jacob and the Indian boy. As she started to run toward the boy, she let out a loud scream: " JOHANN!"

Johann suddenly remembered why Ebenezer was so familiar to him. He had been born here. He ran toward his mother and they came together for a long-overdue, huge hug. Johann was home at last.

11

Jerusalem Lutheran Church

JERUSALEM LUTHERAN CHURCH WAS COMPLETED IN 1769 and is still in use today. It is thought to be Georgia's oldest church. The Ebenezer Orphanage was built soon after, and it too is still standing today. It is now used as a museum.

Before the permanent church was built the congregation worshiped in a hut called a tabernacle and a second wooden church that was built in 1741.

Pastor Boltzius not only served as the church's first pastor for many years, until his death in 1765, but he was also the only judge in Ebenezer. He was given the responsibility for keeping the peace and seeing that the people obeyed the settlement's laws. Much of the recorded history of the Ebenezer settlement was taken from Rev. Boltzius's personal daily journal and historical writings.

Because of the many children left without parents who needed a place to live, an orphanage was the first community

Jerusalem Lutheran church and orphanage

structure built in 1737. It provided a home for widows and orphans as well as a temporary home for pastors and teachers. Before the permanent church could be built, the orphanage was also used as a place of worship on Sunday, a schoolroom on weekdays, and a place for town meetings as needed. In addition to the large downstairs room it had three rooms upstairs. One room was for the boys, another room was for the girls, and the third room housed the widows. It is thought that the widows served as housemothers for the children who shared their home.

The Lutheran settlers were peaceful people and were very faithful to their religion. They trusted God for their salvation and thanked God for his protection during their escape from their old homes in Europe. By 1734, over one thousand Salzburgers had found asylum in Georgia.

The first school at Ebenezer began in 1734. It taught only subjects in the German language for the first five years of its existence.

Teachers were paid semi-annually and had to live by a strict religious code. Parents of the children paid tuition if they were able, and contributions were also taken from the church congregation to support the school.

The first church had seven deacons, who had the responsibility of overseeing all aspects of the church, including the behavior of its members. All scandal and disgraceful conduct were to be avoided. The deacons also managed the financial affairs of the church.

In addition to their secondary education, students were taught catechism in the church on Sundays. The children were very busy as they studied both in church and school and helped with the many tasks of building and maintaining a home in the Ebenezer setting.

As in Savannah the settlers of Ebenezer had hoped to plant Mulberry trees and raise silkworms to provide silk for the rich folk in England. This enterprise was largely unsuccessful, but farmers did well with crops such as corn, potatoes, rice and peas. They also had successful lumber businesses, especially with the pine and cypress trees. They were also able to harvest tar and pitch from the trees.

All in all the families had been very successful in their new homes, and their hard work and holy lives made Ebenezer a good place to live. Even today many of their descendants live successful and happy lives quite near the place where their lives in America began.

12

Pastor Boltzius and the Growth of Ebenezer

THE SUCCESS AND GROWTH OF THE EBENEZER SETTLEMENT AND the lives of the Salzburger congregation were due in part to the leadership of the Lutheran pastor. Pastor Boltzius had been assigned to them from the beginning. He was also responsible for the recorded history of Ebenezer through the daily entries to his journal. Each night before he slept he would faithfully record whatever had happened that day. Some days the news was big, but usually it was news about the daily lives of the people and events that helped to shape their lives.

Catherine and Maria were eyewitnesses to many of these events. One day, as the evening sun was setting, they talked softly about some of the things that touched their hearts. That day they had seen the only remaining member of the Huber family move into the orphanage. Anna Huber was only thirteen, but she had sadly watched this past year as her mother, father and each of her siblings had passed away. She had cared for each of them as they had gotten weaker and weaker with the plague. By now her heart had grown almost immune to grief.

Pastor Boltzius and a lady from the orphanage had helped Anna pack and bring all of her belongings to the orphanage that morning.

Anna would live on the second floor and share a large bedroom with six other orphan girls. Nine boys lived in the boys' section of the second floor and the other side of the floor was reserved for adults. The grown-ups were mostly widows who had been left alone. Some space was left for ladies who might be living there as temporary guests.

The house itself was well made. It was one of the first structures in Ebenezer. It was needed almost immediately as the need for those who were left alone arose.

The widows helped with the children and served as foster caregivers. All together they were like a large family and although they had known much grief there was a lot of love in the home.

Catherine and Maria were teenagers now and had learned to carry their part of the family's work. They also

Pastor Boltzius

helped other families and things that needed to be done in their community.

It was these late afternoon moments of sharing with each other that they most looked forward to. The pine and cypress trees with the hanging gray moss still shaded the homes and grounds. There were many stumps now where the trees had been cut to make room for growth or to be used as firewood during the winter months. The small cemetery had more graves now and almost everyone would visit it from time to time. Usually they would visit the graves of those that they had loved.

There were many more homes now. They were all built alike with the two or three rooms for sleeping and a sitting room in the main part of the house. The kitchen and eating areas were in the back of the main house. There were a few other buildings now, and the newest church was the center of their lives. Not only was it the place for worship on Sundays, but it served as a classroom for the children's school years.

Pastor Boltzius was always on the lookout for people who were needed in Ebenezer. He had secured Dr. Thilo to care for the medical needs of the people. Dr. Thilo was capable as a doctor and a blessing to the people, but it worried Pastor Boltzius constantly that he was not a believer.

Church members like Mrs. Schweighofer took up more

of the pastor's time than he would have liked. She was always asking him for counselling for her own needs and the needs of her children. Her neighbors called her a hypochondriac. She had many unexplainable physical ailments, and she was not ashamed to enjoy the minister's attention.

The people were always on the lookout for tradesmen to come and live in the community. There was a need for a blacksmith, a tailor, and people who worked with or repaired various equipment. As the community grew people with these skills found their homes among the Salzburgers.

Catherine and Maria talked about Pennsylvania. The word was that it was a good place for the newcomers to live. Some who came from London or Germany or other places in Europe stayed in Savannah or one of the smaller communities. Others were just on their way to Pennsylvania or other places in the North.

Some of the people who came were called indentured servants and had to go where their masters went. They had been free but poor when they came to America and had sold themselves as servants for a number of years in order to have the money to buy passage on the ships that now came more often. Those who had the money would make a deal with those who needed it, and they enjoyed having someone at their command in the new world. Sometimes, though, it was hard on the indentured servants as some of the people who bought their time were not kind masters.

Catherine and Maria knew some of the people who had come as indentured servants and they felt really sorry for the ones who had sold themselves to unkind masters. They enjoyed retelling to each other the story they had heard of a young indentured girl who had been treated cruelly. She had secured someone to smuggle her out of the area dressed in men's clothes. As far as the girls knew it was a true story and the girl had arrived safely in Pennsylvania.

Now that Catherine was almost seventeen she began to think seriously about being in love, and that still brought thoughts of Hans. They had been able to go back and forth from Savannah to Ebenezer or from Ebenezer to Savannah about once a year and their feelings were becoming feelings of real love.

13

Grandma Berta's Lonely Secret

GRANDMA BERTA ENJOYED SITTING OUTSIDE HER SMALL HOUSE at the edge of the forest near Salzburg, in Austria. She lived a quiet life, and no one suspected the memories and dreams she carried in her heart. She was very helpful to the other settlers especially by sharing her deep knowledge of the herbs and plants in the area.

In addition to her help with minor illnesses and infections, Grandma was the only midwife in the settlement. Some of the young folks like Catherine she had helped deliver even when they were living back in Salzburg. She possessed a special love for the tiny babies she brought into the world and tried to follow their growth into youth and adulthood.

Sadly, Grandma Berta had been an only child. Both of her parents had died young, and she was alone by the time she became a teenager. She never married, but there was a time in her life when she knew the joy of romantic love.

Perhaps it was the fact that it was a secret, even a forbidden love, that made it feel so intense.

Berta and David had met in the small wooded area that surrounded the village of Salzburg. She had come on her weekly search for the plants and herbs she used, and he was there seeking the solitude and quiet of nature's gift to the area. They both came here often, but somehow their paths had never crossed before.

In spite of her lonely life, Berta was a very pretty young girl. She was shapely and petite, and her dark blue eyes exaggerated the pale completion of her face. People often commented about Berta's beauty, but no young man would come calling at the orphanage where she had been forced to live.

David was taken with Berta's beauty and her soft, kindly voice. It was love at first sight for both of the lonely young people. They made plans to meet often in the shade of the tall pine trees where they expressed their intimate thoughts that gradually turned to words of love.

As their love grew David would plant a soft kiss on Berta's cheek, and then his lips found hers. Neither of them had experienced an intimate physical relationship before, but it was only natural that they found this way to express their deep love for each other.

Berta had been expecting a baby almost four months before she and David were sure about what was happening to them. They continued to meet secretly, but now Berta had moved out of the orphanage to a small house that David had helped her find. She was barely seventeen when she gave birth to the beautiful baby girl that she named Caroline.

Caroline was the most wonderful thing that had ever happened to Berta. She was a beautiful baby with big brown eyes and soft curls around her head. She was a good baby and hardly ever cried. She would stare at one of her parents and coo as she tried to move around her brown homemade crib. She learned fast, and soon the chubby, sweet baby became an amazing, active little girl. David and Berta did not live together, but they spent as much time together as time allowed, and Caroline visited her father and his family every week end.

Berta knew that her love would never desert his child, and she thought she, too, was part of that love and that family group. She was so busy caring for her child and spending precious time with David that she did not notice the small changes that were happening to David.

The Sunday night when David did not walk down to Anna's small house to bring little Caroline home was not as upsetting as one might think. It had happened before, and Berta finally went to sleep with the expectation that she would have her daughter home in the morning.

By the time Wednesday morning arrived, though, a shudder raced through her body and she began to tremble thinking something had happened to her child and her lover. Perhaps one of them had become ill and no one knew how to let her know. Although she had never been to David's home, she put on her nicest dress and headed into town. It was her deepest fear that she would find something amiss when she arrived there.

As fate would have it, Berta was right. There was no one at the vacant white house when she arrived. She collapsed upon the deserted porch and stayed there shivering from the cold and the fear until a kindly hand touched her bare shoulder and gently helped her to her feet. It was David's pastor, whose heart must have broken as he learned how Berta had lost her precious child, but even he did not know how to help her.

The days and nights that followed were too painful to remember now that so much time had gone by, and only Grandma Berta knew that she had once been loved by a man and once she had deeply loved a lovely small child that was her own.

14

Caroline Comes Home

CAROLINE HELD A TIGHT GRIP ON THE SMALL ENVELOPE SHE
had hidden in the pocket of her long cotton dress. She had
begun to wish she had hidden it along with the other important papers she had sealed in a small tin box that was lying under the thick, hard mattress where she slept. This was
the only place she could truly call her own on board the
large sailing ship that was carrying Caroline and 75 others to America.

Many of those on board were part of the crew, who
took turns manning the creaky, weathered ship. It wasn't
new, but had proven over and over again that it was tough
and could stand up to the huge waves that sometimes
threatened to wash over the upper deck of the ship. Caroline and her fellow travellers prayed that those who had
chosen this particular ship had chosen well, and that they
would all be safe.

Caroline was so thankful for the two sisters she had met

in London who were with her on the ship and who were also headed to the new world. They, too, were on their way to a new life, and they would settle down in Savannah with their parents who had preceded their departure by almost a year. Sara Nell and Constance had stayed in England to attend college while their parents had gone ahead to be sure the new home would be a safe place for them to spend their lives and raise their families.

Caroline decided to spend a while alone sitting on one of the round barrels that were scattered around the deck. She felt sure that the sisters would look for her if she had not gone below before the thick, steady door was pulled shut for the night. The door shut out the cold wind and water if a random rainstorm should come up during the night.

Although the ship was crowded, Caroline occasionally found a quiet place to sit and try to sort out the last few weeks that had brought her to this place. She had planned to spend her life in Germany, where her father's family had lived for centuries. She had planned to live with or near her beloved father, who had been her anchor for most of her life. She had only vague, but good, memories of her mother, who she believed had been dead for most of her teen-aged and young adult years.

If it had not been for her father's tragic and sudden

illness, Caroline would still be living the life she and her father had planned for her. She would never forget the fateful evening when her father had called her to his bedside because he needed to talk with her. The talks between Caroline and her father were usually short, happy times when they discussed the good life that they were privileged to live. These were times when they smiled and joked and enjoyed each other's company immensely.

This time, however, her father looked old and pale and had a very sad expression on his face. He began with a confession of having been less than honest about Caroline's mother's death. In fact there had been no death. Instead, after her father had taken Caroline away secretly her mother had become part of a group of Salzburgers and had eventually sailed with them to America.

Caroline's father had sadly admitted how he had kept the child and the mother apart and told Caroline how much her mother had loved her. Since he knew his death would come soon, Caroline's father promised to leave her his vast estate. They both knew that this would enable his daughter to book passage to America if she should be inclined to try to locate her mother there.

Now here she was on the deck of the ship where she had booked passage for America. She had been told that the Salzburgers had landed in Savannah, but had gone further inland to their own settlement in a smaller place known as Ebenezer.

As the moon began to rise and night to quickly fall, the cool night time air reminded Caroline it was time to go below. She slipped around the big door just as the men were coming to close it for the night. While she could still see a little by the dim candlelight she found her bunk bed just below the bunk where Constance was already asleep. She could hear the soft breathing of some of the women who slept nearby and the sad crying of the two babies who were on the trip. Most of the women and children had been assigned to sleep in this large room located below decks. The men and bigger boys had their own space nearer to the bow of the ship. Both areas were very crowded, but no one dared to complain as it was necessary that everyone get along well. They would be here together for the next several weeks before they would arrive in Savannah and be able to leave the old ship.

15

Ebenezer

CAROLINE HELD HER BREATH AS THE RICKETY OLD SHIP rounded the curve on the muddy Savannah River. It seemed that the river had gotten more and more muddy and narrow as they sailed toward Ebenezer. She couldn't help but notice the tremendous difference between her home in Germany and the wilderness she would now be a part of.

Ebenezer was quite small compared to Savannah and a tiny speck compared to London. The giant hardwood trees covered with Spanish moss were beautiful, but a little spooky even in the broad day light.

Caroline was helped as she crossed the gang plank to the shore. Somehow she felt that she was over-dressed in comparison to the few ladies she saw in their long plain dresses. Maybe her mother could help her make new dresses that would help her fit in with the other women and girls in Ebenezer.

There it was, the word she had hidden in her heart since she had left Germany. It was her mother who had been dead to her for most of her life. She trembled as she remembered that her mother was here and that soon they would be together again. She was a little sorry that she had not written to her mother and explained that she was on the way.

The people spoke to Caroline, but they stared at her too. No one knew who she was or where she had come from. It was probably the first time a young lady had come to Ebenezer alone.

The newly built Lutheran Church was wonderful, and the family homes looked very comfortable compared to what she had expected. The lone orphanage was attractive by current standards and looked to be a fine place for the children who had lost their parents. Most of the buildings were shaded by the huge trees, especially those where the moss hung low.

Two young girls noticed Caroline and waved to her. She put on her happiest smile and immediately waved back to them. She learned that their names were Catherine and Maria, and they learned that she was Caroline. After a short conversation, she found the courage to repeat the name "Berta" and waited for their response.

After what seemed like a long time one of the girls whispered "Grandma Berta?" Catherine and Maria did not know that Grandma Berta had given birth to a baby girl long, long ago. They shared the familiar details of Grandma Berta's life since they had gotten to know her back in Germany.

They had not known that Grandma had once been madly in love with a handsome young Catholic man or that she had loved and lost a beautiful little girl. Now that they knew, they remembered all the times she had looked so sad with tears running down her face. She must have been remembering Caroline.

16

Caroline Finds her Mother

THE YOUNG GIRLS LAUGHED AS THEY TOOK CAROLINE'S shaking hand and promised to lead her to her mother. They walked past most of the homes where they and the other people lived. The three girls then came upon a small space that led to a single small cabin under a huge oak tree.

Grandma Berta was always happy to see the girls, and today she was pleased to see a newcomer with them. The new lady seemed a good bit older than the teenaged girls, and she seemed to be completely alone except for them. She was beautiful, with soft brown hair and big brown eyes. Her clothes suggested that she had been well off in her former life, and Grandma was puzzled as to why she would come to Ebenezer. Many years ago Caroline had called her mother "Mum." It was an expression that few people used, but somehow it had been special to Grandma and her child. Caroline seemed as if she would like a hug from Grandma. As the two ladies came together into a special embrace, Grandma thought she heard the young lady breathe the word "Mum."

She gasped and stepped back to look at her new guest. No one said anything for what seemed like a long time, and only Caroline and Grandma Berta knew what was happening in their lives.

When she was able to speak again Grandma spoke one word: "Caroline?"

Caroline nodded happily. Catherine and Maria did not understand. However after they were told the wonderful news, they happily hugged the mother and daughter. The teenagers readily promised to come again tomorrow.

Long into the night, Caroline and Grandma Berta talked and cried and laughed together. Caroline told of her father's death and so many other events that had happened back in Germany. Grandma shared how she had come to be a part of the new settlement and of the many friends that her daughter would meet soon. It was surely a night to remember.

17

The Wedding

THE RAINDROPS ON THE ROOF WERE USUALLY WELCOME AND allowed Catherine to relax and go back to sleep. Many of her chores had to wait until the rain was over. Today, however, bad weather was upsetting for her. Today was Saturday, and tomorrow was Sunday, the day that she and Hans would at last become man and wife.

They were both into their twenties now, and since Hans had moved to Ebenezer a few months ago, they had been able to confirm their true love for each other. They had planned their wedding and were happily expecting a long and happy life together.

Catherine dressed quickly and found something to hold over her head as she ran to the kitchen behind the main house. Her mother had prepared a small breakfast of biscuits and bacon and was busy preparing cakes and salads for the wedding meal the next day. Father was sitting at the kitchen table waiting for his daughter to talk with him. They were expecting Hans to arrive by midmorning to go over the final wedding plans.

This afternoon there would be a wedding reception for the young couple at the main floor of the orphanage. Friends and neighbors would help with the food for the reception, and some of them would bring presents for the bride and groom. Tomorrow afternoon after church they would have Rev. Boltzius lead the short wedding ceremony uniting the couple in marriage.

Catherine and Hans were happy to take time to talk with their best friends Maria and her husband Andrew. They were at the orphanage helping with the arrangement of the food and the final decorations for the reception. Maria and Andrew had been married about a year and were expecting their first baby in a few months. Andrew had come from Germany with his family to settle in Ebenezer a few years ago.

It was a happy time in the new world. By now many people had arrived from Europe and the settlements along the Savannah River and those farther to the west of the river were growing rapidly.

Occasionally they received news from the northern English colonies. Some of the people who had come through Ebenezer had gone on to make their homes in Pennsylvania.

By early afternoon the sun was shining and raindrops were glistering on the grass and flowers in front of the orphanage. Catherine was dressed in her prettiest new dress except for the white one she had planned to wear for her wedding. Hans, too, was in his nicest Sunday clothes. He would wear them again for the service. Maria had brushed Catherine's hair for a long time and added a pretty pink ribbon to match the new dress.

Maria and Andrew, who were to be the maid of honor and the best man for the wedding stood beside Catherine and Hans in the receiving line and welcomed the guests. Both of their mothers stood at the refreshment tables and thanked their friends and neighbors for coming. It was a long afternoon of merriment and happiness, especially for the young couple and their families.

Toward the end of the reception Catherine and Hans sat near the front of the room and took turns opening the pretty gifts that their friends had brought to help them set up a home of their own.

After the guests had left, Hans, too, went home with his parents. He had given Catherine a soft kiss and a tight hug with "See you tomorrow, my love."

Catherine's head was filled with memories and antici-
pation, and it was hard for her to sleep. She strained to remember the happy days she and her family had lived back
in Austria over a decade ago. The long hard trip from Austria to London stood out in her memory as did the eight
weeks of following the setting sun on the Atlantic Ocean.
Those days, as well as the first few years in America, had
been hard and brought sad memories. She thought of the
people who had died and friends she had lost. She missed
them terribly, but she would not let these memories ruin
her joy at her wedding.

Sunday morning came quietly, and all the family was
up early cleaning and dressing for the church service that
would be followed by the wedding service. Father went out
into the yard and into the woods to pick the prettiest flowers that had been chosen for vases in the church.

By the time the ten o'clock service began, Catherine
was sitting on the front row with her family, and Hans was
in the back row with his family. They were not allowed to
see each other until it was time for the wedding to begin.

It seemed that Rev. Boltzius would never finish his ser-
mon and even the hymns and prayers lasted longer than
they usually did. Catherine wiggled in her seat, and she
was happy to turn aside and see that General Oglethorpe

and Tomochichi had made it to the service and would stay for the wedding. They had been very special friends for the Salzburgers since they had arrived from London.

As soon as the service ended everyone shifted in their seats, and some of the rows of benches were turned sideways to make room for the wedding party and the pastor.

It was such a happy time when Catherine and Hans accompanied by Maria and Andrew rose to stand together in front of the pastor and all of their family and friends. They listened carefully and repeated reverently the vows as the pastor read them. Almost as soon as the service had begun, it seemed, they heard the pastor speak the words, "I now pronounce you man and wife. You may kiss your bride."

It was a nice soft kiss and gentle hug as the young couple looked happily forward to the many years to come as husband and wife.

The cemetery at Ebenezer

18

Time Goes On

TIME GOES ON. CATHERINE, HANS, MARIA, ANDREW AND Caroline went on with their lives, growing up and having families of their own. They will live forever in the world of fiction.

Johann eventually came home to live with his real family. He, however, maintained a relationship with his Indian mother.

Anna Huber was a real person although her name may have been changed. She can be found today in Heaven and her body lies with the real Salzburgers in the Ebenezer Cemetery. She was remembered because she lost all of her family and grew up in the Ebenezer Orphanage.

Of course Oglethorpe, Tomochichi, and Pastor Boltzius were real people who live today in Heaven and in the American History books.

The Salzburgers, too, live on in the lives of their descendants---In the churches and schools of Effingham County. We find there the following families and many more: Shearouse, Zeigler, Seckinger, Rahn, Arnsdorff, Kessler, Exley, Keiffer, Zitterouer, Reiser, Gnann, and Zoller.

May God Bless the Salzburgers of Ebenezer. May He especially bless those who bravely followed the setting sun so long ago.

About the Author

LUCY MORGAN WALLER was
born and raised in Fayet-
teville, Georgia. She is the
proud mother of four grown
children and grandmother
of four grandchildren. She
spent 25 years as a Baptist
pastor's wife and 30 years as
an elementary school teach-
er. Since retiring, she is an

active member of her church, where she teaches Sunday
School, works in the church office, and shares her faith with
others at every opportunity. When she is not spending time
with her family and friends, she enjoys finally having the time
to pursue her writing. Follow the Setting Sun is her third
book. Lucy incorporates her sense of humor and interest
in history in her books, as well as in her occasional speech-
es. Lucy considers God and family as her top priorities.

25438425R00058

Made in the USA
San Bernardino, CA
30 October 2015